Pete the Cat

Rock On, Mom and Dad!

by
James Dean

HARPER FESTIVAL
An Imprint of HarperCollinsPublishers

Harperfestival is an imprint of HarperCollins Publishers.

Pete the Cat: Rock On, Mom and Dad!
Copyright © 2015 by James Dean. All rights reserved.
Manufactured in China.
For information address HarperCollins Children's Books,
a division of HarperCollins Publishers, 195 Broadway, New York, NY 10007.
www.harpercollinschildrens.com

Library of Congress catalog card number: 2013956492
ISBN 978-0-06-230408-7

Book design by Jeanne Hogle
14   15   16   17   18   LEO   10   9   8   7   6   5   4   3   2   1
❖
First Edition

It's Monday morning, and Pete the Cat is late for school. His alarm didn't go off.

Does Pete have to worry? Not at all.

Dad has made
him breakfast.

Mom has packed
his backpack.

Pete is even going to make the bus!

Pete knows that Mom and Dad do so much for him.

Mom helps him practice baseball.

Dad takes him to his guitar lessons.

Every day, Mom and Dad do a hundred little things. And Pete realizes that he's never really said thank you.

Today Pete is going to surprise Mom and Dad
with something totally awesome.

But what should he do?

He could make them
breakfast in bed.

He could pick them a bouquet of flowers.

He could clean the house . . .

or mow the lawn . . .

or change the oil in Dad's car.

That all seems nice, but it doesn't seem like enough.

Pete really wants to do something
that they'll never ever forget.

Pete talks to his big brother, Bob.
Bob is the smartest guy he knows.

"What can I do to tell Mom and Dad how much I love them?" Pete asks.

"It doesn't matter what you do,"
Bob says. "It's how you do it.

"So long as it's from the heart,
Mom and Dad will totally dig it."

That gives Pete an idea.
There is one thing Pete
can do better than any
other cat he knows. . . .

So Pete writes Mom and Dad a song,
and it goes a little something like this:

Mom and Dad, you are the best. I love you more than all the rest— Yeah I do.

I cannot count all the things you do.
I know it's all **because of you**—
Yes it is—
That I love music and I love art

And I love you with all my heart. Yes I do.

It is the best surprise ever!